Mouse's Best Day Ever

by the same author

The Mouse's House
Children's Reflexology for Bedtime or Anytime
Susan Quayle
Illustrated by Melissa Muldoon
Foreword by Barbara Scott
ISBN 978 1 84819 247 8
eISBN 978 0 85701 193 0

of related interest

Seahorse's Magical Sun Sequences
How all children (and sea creatures) can use yoga to feel positive, confident and completely included
Michael Chissick
Illustrated by Sarah Peacock
ISBN 978 1 84819 283 6
eISBN 978 0 85701 230 2

Connor the Conker and the Breezy Day
An Interactive Pilates Adventure
Rachel Lloyd
Foreword by Alan Watson
ISBN 978 1 84819 294 2
eISBN 978 0 85701 244 9

Baby Shiatsu
Gentle Touch to Help Your Baby Thrive
Karin Kalbantner-Wernicke and Tina Haase
Illustrated by Monika Werneke
Foreword by Steffen Fischer
ISBN 978 1 84819 104 4
eISBN 978 0 85701 086 5

Mouse's Best Day Ever

CHILDREN'S REFLEXOLOGY TO SOOTHE SORE TEETH AND TUMS

SUSAN QUAYLE
ILLUSTRATED BY MELISSA MULDOON
FOREWORDS BY SPIROS DIMITRAKOULAS AND SALLY EARLAM

SINGING
DRAGON
LONDON AND PHILADELPHIA

First published in 2016
by Singing Dragon
an imprint of Jessica Kingsley Publishers
73 Collier Street
London N1 9BE, UK
and
400 Market Street, Suite 400
Philadelphia, PA 19106, USA

www.singingdragon.com

Library of Congress Cataloging in Publication Data
A CIP catalog record for this book is available from the Library of Congress

British Library Cataloguing in Publication Data
A CIP catalogue record for this book is available from the British Library

ISBN 978 1 84819 315 4
eISBN 978 0 85701 269 2

Printed and bound in China

For Francis Edward Quayle, 1937–2002.
SQ

For Mum and Dad – thanks for everything.
MM

Contents

Foreword

As a parent I wish the day had more than 24 hours, maybe then I could find the time needed to express my love to my children, even to my wife. Unfortunately, the day does not have more hours, but thankfully I am a reflexologist and a massage therapist!

I utilise this simple yet effective knowledge through touch, positive intention and presence and top it off with love at bedtime, hoping to make up for time. It seems to be working!

For you – the parent who wishes to express their love and caring, and to create unbreakable bonds with their children that will be encrypted on a cellular level – this book is the aid.

Besides helping you to create bonds, this book can also be used to help calm down your child for bedtime and from stress in general; it is a means to teach your children about their body; it might even prove to be a worthy complement to address illnesses or pursue wellbeing.

Lastly, a benefit you might have not thought of is to decrease any possible aggression your child has. This is verified by promising anti-bullying programmes going on around the world.

We all came to this world with the knowledge and intention to offer positive touch. Let us use this book to cultivate it in our children and heal the world.

Spiros Dimitrakoulas (Σπύρος Δημητράκουλας)
Chair of Reflexology in Europe Network
October 2015

Foreword

I am so delighted to see the return of Mouse and am sure that you and your child are looking forward to sharing in another adventure. Setting time aside to read to our children is a precious part of parenting and the adventure of Mouse has a remarkable twist to its tale. The book brings together a fun read with beautiful illustrations, combined with simple reflexology moves to improve health and calm fractious minds.

Seeing the benefits of reflexology in my own son and daughter led me to work as a reflexologist with many children over the years, from babies through to teenagers. I never cease to be amazed by the power of this therapy.

I trust this enchanting book will be the start of a journey into health, happiness and reflexology for both you and your child.

Sally Earlam FMAR. BSc. RN. PGCE
Head of Training and Education for
the Association of Reflexologists
Board Member of the Reflexology
in Europe Network

This Children's Reflexology Programme has been designed to enable parents, family and friends to offer children the benefits of reflexology in a way that is fun, relaxing and supports natural bonding.

Reflexology is a gentle, non-invasive complementary therapy that can help with many common ailments of childhood. The feet contain reflex points that correspond to different parts of the body. When these reflexes are manipulated it helps to ease problems within that area of the body and support the body's own ability to self-heal. As a reflexologist I have worked with many babies, toddlers and children, as well as adults, and have seen how effective it can be.

As well as offering invaluable therapeutic benefits, this book is designed to aid the bonding process between the adult and child. Reading this story at bedtime and performing the actions on the child's foot will create a sense of quality time, fun and positive touch between you. The time you spend relating this story in a positive way will offer help, distraction, comfort and a feeling of safety at other times in your child's life. In my experience children can be brought back from utter distress with a comforting distraction that is familiar to them.

It is also a way for parents to offer help at times when they feel helpless. A child suffering in pain from a condition such as constipation, colic or teething is heart-breaking for a parent who feels unable to offer any relief. With these stories there is the opportunity not only to help comfort them but to actually help relieve their discomfort.

Repeated regularly, this story can help to support your child's good health. It can also offer you the chance to catch a problem before it develops and becomes out of control. Regular treatments can relieve conditions such as constipation, colic and teething before they become a problem. Reflexology can also be used to work alongside conventional medicine to support more serious conditions such as asthma and epilepsy.

As a complementary therapist I would never encourage anyone to stop taking prescribed medication unless it had been sanctioned by their doctor.

The Gentle Touch

When working on very young children – newborns, babies and toddlers – it is essential that you use a very light touch. Their young feet are very sensitive. Their bones and musculature will be undeveloped and their reflexes will be very sensitive. It is unlikely that you will hurt your child, unless you use a very strong pressure, but it will not be conducive to the relaxing and positive results we are after. Never perform reflexology on a child when you are feeling angry, as it is important that the experience remains a positive one for everyone, especially them.

Basic Reflexology Techniques

Caterpillar

The caterpillar, or thumb and finger walking, will be the most used technique. The illustration shows thumb walking. Slide the tip of the thumb forward by extending the first joint as shown, then raise the joint to the original position by rolling the tip of the thumb in place, and repeat. The tip will move slowly forward in very small steps like a caterpillar walking. Finger walking is very similar but uses the index finger instead of the thumb.

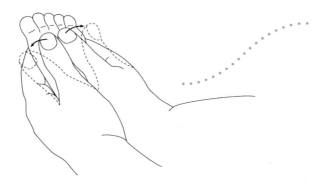

Butterfly

This is done using the outside edge of both thumbs to gently stroke the reflex, pulling away from each other. Useful when working the Lung reflex. Hold the foot as shown in the image and stroke the reflex gently by moving the thumbs apart. Lift the thumbs and return them to the original position to repeat.

Finger Stroking

This is basically what it says. Use a gentle motion with a light pressure, stroking the foot downwards with the fingers.

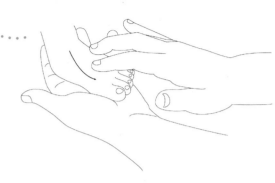

Hand Stroking

Gently glide your hands, palms down, over the feet, completely enveloping them with the warmth and comfort of your hands. Glide up the foot toward the leg and then down the sides before starting over. Very relaxing and a lovely way to begin and end the story.

Kissing

This is your baby, grandchild or little person that you care for. Add a nurturing dimension with kissing and playing and silliness. Bring love and play into the story. Use puppets, toys and funny voices. There are no rules – do what you need to do to make it work for you and your child. To begin with, just get them used to having their feet touched throughout the story. There is no hurry, you have their whole childhood ahead of you. Whatever happens is OK, as long as your intention is positive.

The Story and How to Use This Book

This story is based around a group of animal characters. The intention is that each animal represents a particular reflex area. The central character in this book is Mouse. She represents the Solar Plexus, which is very important in all conditions related to pain, discomfort, stress and anxiety.

Each page of the story has a diagram of the feet at the top of the page showing the reflexes that you should be working, with written instructions on what to do. This story will provide a reflexology treatment to help when your child is suffering with teething and colic in babies, and toothache, headaches and stress-related stomach aches in older children. This means that the reflexes relating to these conditions will be manipulated if you follow the instructions alongside the foot maps on each page. There are hundreds of ways in which stories can be used to aid children, and this one has another dimension to add to its value. I hope you have fun with it.

If you are using this book with young children, say between one and three years old, you might find it easier to just read it to them as a story at first. This allows the child (and you) to become familiar with the story and the characters. Children in this age group often find it difficult to sit still and may be resistant to having their feet touched initially. You might like to try just holding their feet while you read the story before progressing on to manipulating the reflexes. Don't give up. If they need the treatment for a condition you can give them the reflexology while they are sleeping until they are ready to receive it while awake. Try not to force them to sit and have the treatment if they are not interested as it may create a barrier to future enjoyment. Some of the young children who have experienced this book were resistant in the beginning but all of them loved it after a very short time.

When using the book with babies, including newborns, try to read the story while giving the treatment. Using a sing song voice with a variety of pitches will soothe and calm the baby. In my experience, babies respond positively to warmth and love so make this the intention when reading. Have fun above all else.

The Reflexes and Characters

The characters in this book each represent a reflex area of the foot. As you visit each of the reflexes, the character representing that reflex appears in the story.
  Here are the characters you will meet.

Mouse
Mouse represents the
Solar Plexus reflex point.

Squirrel
Squirrel represents the Head,
Sinus, Teeth, Eyes and
Ear reflexes.

Hare
Hare represents the Lungs
and Chest reflexes.

Mole
Mole represents the
Digestive System reflexes.

Otter
Otter represents the
Lymphatic System reflex.

Snake
Snake represents the
Nervous System, Back
and Spine reflexes.

Mouse's Best Day Ever

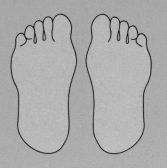

Gently hand stroke your child's feet to prepare them for their reflexology treatment.

In the ocean blue and deep
Sat an island chain that looked like feet
Joined together with toes of trees
That gently sighed in the salty breeze

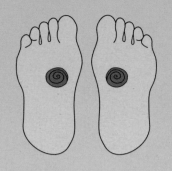

Gently hold with thumbs.

Warm and cosy in her nest
Mouse was waking from her rest
When the door was opened wide
And Mole erupted from outside

"Remember we're supposed to be
having tea in Squirrel's tree"
Mouse jumped up and said to Mole
"Hurray! I'm up, come on, let's go!"

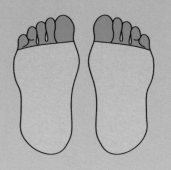

Gently caterpillar
walk up the toes.

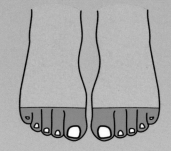

Gently caterpillar walk
down the toes.

Gently circle the
tops of the toes.

Squirrel met them at the door
And led them to the highest floor
Up the spiral stairs inside
To the tree tops spreading wide

As they looked into the room
Mouse was filled with fear and doom
The floor was moving with the trees
Blowing gently in the breeze

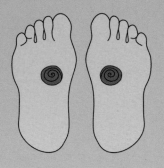

Gently hold with thumbs.

Mouse quite often felt afraid
And had a little game she played
She'd think about her cosy nest
Where she felt safe and loved to rest

Feeling better straight away
Determined to enjoy her day
She smiled at both her friends and said
"I'll be right there, you go ahead"

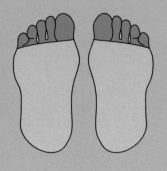

Gently caterpillar walk up the toes.

Floating in the canopy
Was a table set for three
Scones with acorn cream and jam
Chestnuts, hot, with apple flan

Squirrel said, "It's time to eat
Fill your plate and grab a seat"
Mouse and Mole sat down with glee
Ate everything, washed down with tea

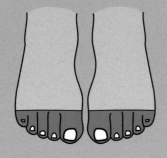

Gently caterpillar walk down the toes.
Gently circle the tops of the toes.

As they ate and talked away
The wind blew hard; the branches swayed
Rain clouds came, the sun went in
The rustling leaves set up a din

Looking for a place to hide
Squirrel took poor Mouse inside
Tea things piled upon a tray
Mole came in all wan and grey

Gently caterpillar
walk up the toes.

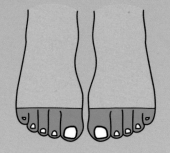

Gently caterpillar walk
down the toes.

Gently circle the
tops of the toes.

The wind and rain became a storm
The friends were feeling scared, forlorn
They stood and watched the tree room sway
Sad their day should end this way

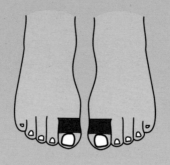

Gently slide your finger down the top of the big toe.

With a disappointed groan
Mole thought he would just go home
An idea popped into his head
Jumping up he smiled and said

"Oh no! The day's not over yet
Come to mine, it won't be wet"
So off they set to go to Mole's
Down one of his many holes

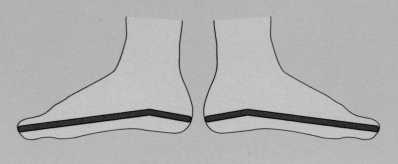

Gently caterpillar walk down the inside of the foot. Slowly work your way back using tiny gentle circular movements.

Curled up on his flowery floor
Snake heard voices at his door
Popping out to say hello
The friends all jumped and cried out, "OH!"

"Did I sscare you? Sssorry," he said
"I wass jusst about to go to bed"
"You did!" said Mole. "We're off to play
At mine, out of this stormy day"

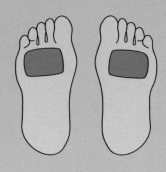

Gently caterpillar walk or butterfly stroke, thumbs together stroking outward.

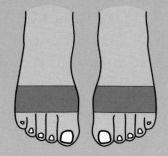

Gently caterpillar walk from the base of the toe down the foot, or butterfly stroke, thumbs together stroking outward.

"Come and join us Snake," said Mole
"There's plenty of space for us below"
Snake said, "Yess I'd love to come
Let'ss all go and have ssome fun"

They could hear Hare running, thumping the ground
As they went through the tunnels earthy and round
There were so many rooms, deep, cosy and warm
Soon they forgot the blustery storm

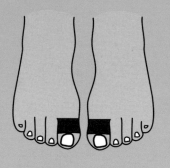

Gently slide your finger down the top of the big toe.

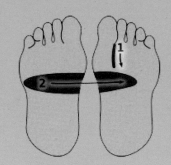

1. Gently slide your thumb down from the join between the big and second toes.

2. Starting on the right foot, slide your thumb across from right to left.

"Let's all play a game!" they cried
"There's lots of places for us to hide"
They laughed and played, had tons of fun
Until they had a rumbling tum

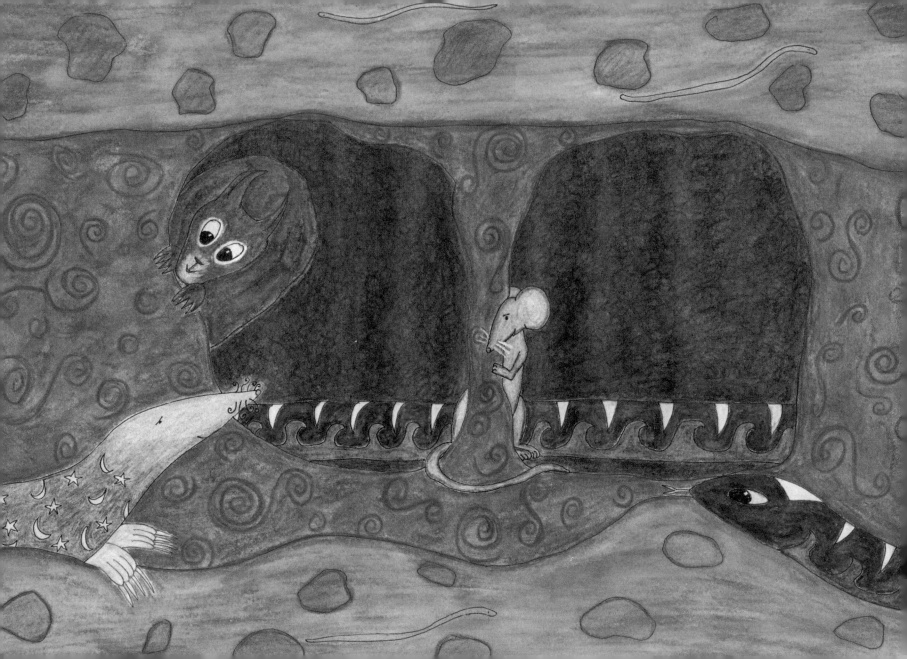

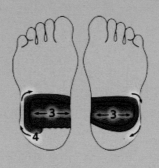

3. Butterfly stroke the lower centre of each foot.

4. Starting on the right foot, gently caterpillar walk or use tiny circles to follow the horseshoe.

Mole took them down to the kitchen to eat
Together they cooked up delicious treats
Potatoes in jackets with buttery greens
Summery berries with golden ice-cream

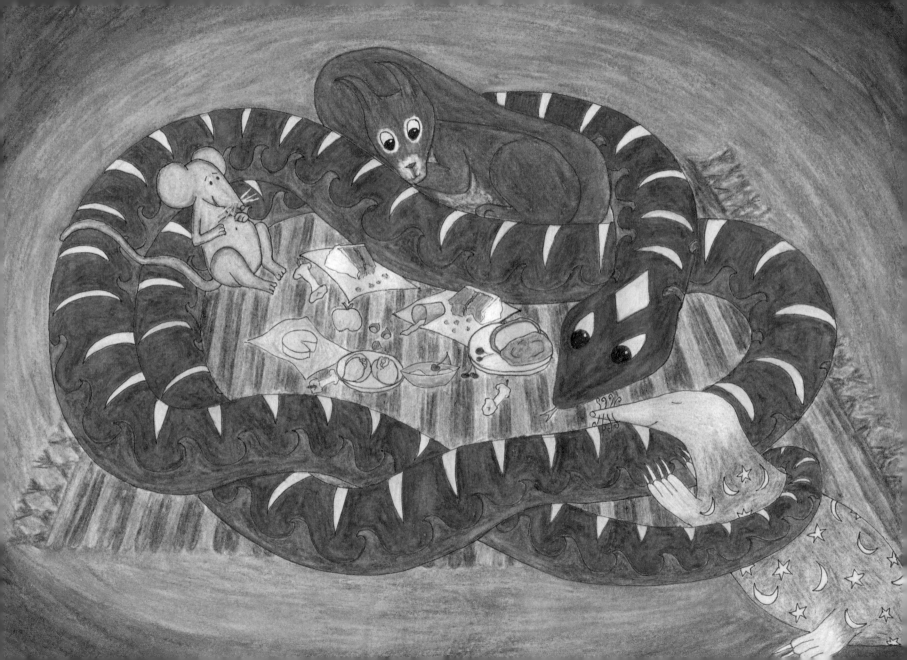

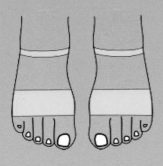

Caterpillar walk from the base of the toes down the top of the foot. Butterfly stroke the top of the foot.

Gently using tiny circles, work your way around the top of the ankle, gently stroking up the leg.

Mole said, "Let's see if the storm's moved on"
They went to the surface and saw it was gone
A huge full moon in a dark velvet sky
Hung over the ocean as Otter swam by

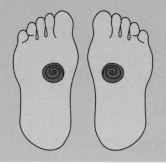

Gently hold with thumbs.

All feeling tired, the day had been long
They ended the night with a last moonlit song
As together they took Mouse home to her bed
"That was the best day ever," they said

The Children's Reflexology Programme

Since the publication of *The Mouse's House* I have been busy creating The Children's Reflexology Programme (TCRP). This began as a course that I taught to parents so they could learn basic reflexology techniques to use on their children and families at home, anytime, much like the book. The courses were such a big hit that I felt all parents should have access to it, so I have created an additional course that teaches people to be instructors so they can teach parents. This course is open to anyone who has a healthy interest in supporting parents and children. It is my intention to reach as many children as I can and share the good news about this gentle yet powerful complementary therapy.

Over the last year I have travelled across the country creating instructors and spreading the word. The course is now officially recognised by the Association of Reflexologists and the Federation of Holistic Therapists. This means you can be reassured that the course is considered to be of a very high standard. If you would like to run your own ethical business supporting parents by sharing these gentle techniques please do get in touch. If you are a new mum or dad who feels that you don't want to go back to your job but would like to build a business around your family then this course has been created with you in mind. Start small and slowly and let your business grow with your child. You will have a constant supply of parents around you that you can reach and teach.

If you are older and your children have all left home and you would like to reconnect with young mums and their children, this could be for you too. Whoever you are and whatever your reasons, this is a lovely way to bring people together, to support parents with young children and to connect with your own communities.

To find out more about TCRP please visit our website at www.kidsreflex.co.uk.